Copyright © 2007 by NordSüd Verlag AG, Zürich, Switzerland
First published in Switzerland under the title *Inga zieht sich an*
English translation copyright © 2007 by North-South Books Inc., New York

First published in the United States, Great Britain, Canada, Australia, and New
Zealand in 2007 by North-South Books Inc., an imprint of NordSüd Verlag AG,
Zürich, Switzerland. Distributed in the United States by North-South Books Inc.,
New York.

Library of Congress Cataloging-in-Publication Data is available.
A CIP catalogue record for this book is available from The British Library.

ISBN-13: 978-0-7358-2128-6 / ISBN-10: 0-7358-2128-3 (trade edition)
10 9 8 7 6 5 4 3 2 1

Printed in Belgium

For Nils and Regina

I Can Dress Myself!

By Birte Müller

Translated by Marianne Martens

NORTHSOUTH
BOOKS
New York / London

It was a beautiful day, just right for a trip to the park.

"Come on, Daisy," Mother said. "I'll help you get dressed, and then we can go to the playground."

"Yay!" answered Daisy. "I'll bring Rootie, too. But I don't need help. I can dress *myself*."

Daisy knew exactly what she wanted to wear. Her favorite flowery summer dress.

"No, Daisy, that dress is too thin. It's a little chilly outside," said Mother. Her voice sounded very firm. Daisy knew there was no point in arguing with her.

"Why don't you wear your red overalls? They look so cute on you," said Mother.

"No, thanks. I'll dress *myself*."

"Could I at least help you find something?" asked Mother.

"No, thanks, Rootie will help me," said Daisy, sounding very firm herself.

Mother knew there was no point in arguing with her.

Daisy and Rootie looked in the closet.
"I'll wear the purple dress. My pink purse
will match it beautifully," decided Daisy.

"Noooooooo!" squeaked Rootie. "I hate purple.
It's a disgusting color," she whined. "Don't
you have any orange clothes? I love orange."

Daisy thought of her orange hooded sweatshirt.
"Mootherrrr! Where's my orange sweatshirt with
the white polka dots?" she shouted.
"It's wet and hanging on the clothesline," called Mother.

"Why don't you wear your green checked pants? Green is a lovely color," suggested Rootie.

"Because they don't fit anymore," said Daisy. Rootie insisted that she try them on. But Daisy was right—they were really much too small.

"Too bad!" said Rootie, disappointed. She liked checks.

"I know. I'll wear my blue striped pants!"
said Daisy, slipping them on.

"They're much too big," said Rootie. And she was right.

Daisy had another idea. The blue sweater that Grandma
had knit for her would be perfect.

When she couldn't find it, she ran into the kitchen
to ask Mother.

"Sweetheart, the blue sweater is at Grandma's
house. She was going to mend it for you," said Mother,
whose voice was starting to sound a little cranky.

"Why don't you just put on your beige jacket,"
said Mother impatiently.

"No, thanks, I'll dress myself," said Daisy,
slamming her door angrily.

Now Mother was mad. "Well, hurry up! You
have one more minute. If you aren't dressed . . ."
said Mother.

"I'm ready! But Rootie can't decide what she wants to wear!"

"Hmmmm," said Mother. "If Rootie can't make up her mind, then she'll have to stay at home. And that's that!"

"You heard Mother, Rootie," said Daisy firmly.
"You're going to put on your green pants *right now!*
Otherwise you're not coming to the playground. And that's
that."

Daisy grabbed her bucket. "We're both dressed, Mother!"
she said. And they all went to the playground.